TOO MANY MOUTHS TO FEED

Jennifer Skyers

Published Independently

ISBN-13 979-8418111968
ASIN: B095L2T49C

All the characters in the book are fictitious and any resemblance to actual persons, living or dead, is purely coincidental.

Chapter 1

Home Life

On a steep windy path and down a hill stands a large stone exterior house where the Harrodian family reside. This includes Charles and Sarah Harrodian, their two children Rupert and George and another one on the way.

For the Harrodians, home is situated in an idyllic setting in Cornwall surrounded by the sea. As a family, they spent most of their time in a three-storey townhouse in Windsor, their father's choice, so that his children could be in London for schooling, and it also meant that travel wasn't too much of a problem for his work. In the long recess of the summer holidays, the family spent long, hazy sunny days in Cornwall where they got to unwind, relax and have fun. If they didn't travel abroad, then Charles their father, made it his priority to join the rest of the family for his allotted summer break from work in Cornwall. Outside of these times, the house was usually rented to holidaymakers who came into the area for short breaks and also for businesses needing accommodation for residential courses and such like. There was also an occasional cook and hired help.

My mother and father are pillars of the community as my father is the Head Bursary of the local public school and somewhat part-time stockbroker for the highly acclaimed stockbrokers, Silverkin. His wife Sarah, my mother, qualified as a teacher but has chosen to remain at home after the birth of her first son to raise the family. They live well and enjoy the finer things in life. They had insisted in continuing the long held family tradition of privately educating their children and have already reserved places for the youngest of their children at Harrow and Roedean respectively.

Born into a comfortable family we have been fortunate as we have been able to establish impeccable connections as my grandfather had worked in the Royal Cavalry for a time. His cousin, on his father's side, married Lady Esquith of Berkshire. Because of this, we have the privilege of attending many a party and royal bash.

Life is fun with weekends away fishing or hunting with well connected friends. I was lucky that my family had such good friends who had children my age, fifteen, and in my final year at school. I have plans for life after school. I remember thinking that I certainly didn't want to see active service on the front line, but I was happy to help out in the munitions factory, which I see as my way of contributing to the war effort. More importantly however, I have plans to become a doctor and luckily for me, I have secured a place at Cambridge to pursue my studies.

My father took a weekly and a daily paper and in recent days there had been a lot written in the papers about war breaking out in Austria. Indeed, the papers provided a detailed account of the invasion in Sarajevo and the subsequent assassination of Archduke Franz Ferdinand. Germany came to the aid of Austria and offered their army and support. Provoked by France's political clout and its allegiance with Britain, which has the greatest naval force in the world, Germany invaded France hoping to gain political advantages. Once France had been invaded, Britain had no choice but to join them because they were allies. I remember thinking that if war breaks out it would change the face of Britain and the political landscape.

War is declared

My father sent me to buy a copy of the Guardian. I was fifteen, all of FIFTEEN, and grown up. I loved going to collect the papers as it meant being able to treat myself with the change left from the money given. There was always the latest comic that mother sometime had overlooked to buy, so by going to the newsagent I was able to furnish and maintain my library stock of comics.

Lots of people were thronging the open market area peering over their newspapers. Rupert hurried along into the newsagent to pick up his copy. What was all the fuss about – what had got the people chatting so animatedly he mused within himself? He quickened his footsteps and pushed his way into the store, nearly tripping over Tommy the ginger cat who had nestled himself in the corner of the doorway as per usual.

'Good day Mr. Cooper,' Rupert said politely. 'May I have a copy of today's Guardian please.'

'Here you are young boy,' Mr. Cooper said as he exchanged a copy of the paper for the sum of 2d. 'Yes boy, you will see that they have declared war on us here; what will become of us?' said Mr. Cooper gesturing with his hands as he pointed to the article splashed on the front page.

The paper read thus:

'With the utmost reluctance and with infinite regret, His Majesty's Government have been compelled to place this country in a state of war with what for many years and indeed many generations past has been a friendly power.'

The Guardian went on to report that Britain had braced the country to go to war to preserve and vindicate and defend the principle of ally kinship as Germany had stoked the flames of war and had declared war on the Russia/Austrian pact.

Later that evening as the Harrodian family sat at dinner, the chimes of Big Ben rang out as was the hourly custom but this time it seemed the bells tolled to proclaim the fact that war had been declared.   The chimes rang out in echo to the announcement made by the government led by Prime Minister Herbert Henry Asquith.

Boom!

The deep notes of Big Ben rang out into the night, the first strokes that sounded out in Britain since the announcement in the paper proclaiming that Britain was at war.

Boom! Boom! Boom! The last stroke sounded and then silence fell..........................

No-one spoke for a while. It was as if they were trying to articulate into words what the impact of war would mean on the family unit; the Sunday walks, the holidays abroad, the quiet times spent reading with the children. The faces of the family as they sat at dinner spoke volumes but a single word was yet to be uttered. Rupert then broke the silence with a question.

'What if it all ends badly and there are many wounded.'

Sarah whispered quietly, 'what will become of us?'

'Mummy, why do we have to go to war – it's not our fight?' George piped up. His voice sounded tinny as he was still passing through puberty and his voice had not yet fully broken into the velvet deep auburn tones which seemed to pervade all the men in the Harrodian household, even his older brother. Sometimes one could forget that despite George being a tall chap, he was still a young boy mentally and in the early stages of puberty and as such, still had an enquiring mind and lots of unanswered questions which he would sometimes just randomly throw out there.

Charles placed his hand comfortingly on George's shoulder and proceeded. 'Britain is like a family to France and the Belgians,' Charles said. 'In instances of major concern, we as a country do like a good family would do if a member of the family were facing a crisis; we would come to the aid of those in need and offer our support. The Belgium borders are close to our own and we need to stave off a potential threat from Germany who have declared war on Russia,' continued Charles.

'Oh I see,' George said. 'Does this mean that you will have to go to war too? Could you object and stay around to help with the new baby when it arrives?' questioned George.

The children had lots of questions and it was like a fiery question and answer session which Charles took upon himself to anchor. In the end, and as an answer to all answers, Charles said, 'the good Lord will look after us all.'

There had already been rumours of war and the community were quite jittery and had spent much of the last seven days or so huddled together in the public houses discussing the prospect of the breakout of war. But now it was a reality. Britain at war would mean that the fit and able men of Great Britain would be galvanized together to help assist with defending and protecting their allies. Instead of the foreboding fear and sadness with which the news was initially received by the Harrodian family, the atmosphere on the street and in the community, by contrast, was quite different. The news was received to cheers and shouts of 'long live the King' and 'Rule Britannia.'

Rupert reflected on the fact that all around him in the streets and in the homes of families he visited, there was a palpable sense of duty and sobriety as the seriousness of the scale of the war, (being dubbed the 'Great War' by many), became clear to not only the people of his community but also to the people of Britain as a whole. A new war generation had been birthed. A war of this scale meant that every eligible male could be called up at any time and be conscripted into the army to fight to defend the honour of the Great Empire. War had now been declared.

Chapter 2

Preparing for War

My father Charles was a deep-thinking person having inherited a head for politics and social affairs from his own father and was a member of the Brogue Men's Club, aptly and affectionately named because of the love of brogue shoes worn by many members of the group, largely men of a certain age. They would often come round in the evening and talk into the small hours of the morning about anything that featured in the headlines that day; some of the group worked with Charles. Thereafter, the conversation on the street was invariably the same.

'Chitter chatter ....'

'Chitter chatter ....'

'Mumble mumble...'

'Grumble grumble...'

The crowds found nothing else to talk about but the war and the reasons for it. One thing for sure was the consensus of opinion amongst the gentleman of the day, and here I am referring to the men of the day, those suited and booted with stiff white collars worn under woollen tweed suits.

War was inevitable because of the increasing competition and desire for greater empires which led to the confrontation that helped push the world into World War One with each country vying for dominance and power and to prove their influence. This was one of the theories being debated and so as time went on it was clear to all that the war would extend to include all of Europe with the various allies emerging thereby bringing the whole world into the war to protect nationalism and pride. Fifteen million dead and twenty million injured. What a price to pay for national pride!

Many men volunteered their support and joined the army. I had already decided that if I was approached, I would stake my right as a conscientious objector, but moreover, surely I would be needed at home to help out with family life. I could always decline to join the army and instead offer my support in the munitions factory after school. Anyway, all things considered, I had the opportunity to go to university at the age of eighteen and so my focus was on doing just that.

On a cold but sunny day in November, (I remember it well), my father called the family together and told us that he had signed up for the war and that he would be leaving the family home to undergo training in Aldershot. The news was received solemnly as it was the first time that we had really ever been apart from one another. However, despite the solemnity of the occasion, one could not help but feel a tinge of excitement because it wasn't just an ordinary event; Daddy would be fighting for King and country and there was also the respect and honour that came with it. But then there was the down side to consider too, one which we as a family had already lingered over and this related to the inevitable casualties of war and the fear of never seeing your loved ones again. My father was joining the largest training force ever to be mobilized as it had been reported that over thirty million men had been mobilized to fight in the First World War.

After thirteen months of progressive training, Charles Harrodian joined the thousands of soldiers enlisted to fight in the war as Sergeant Harrodian on the 14th of February 1916.

For all the camaraderie and fighting talk, the war brought severe hardship and economic discontent to England and this included friends of our family too. Basic food items were in short supply and my mother had a fine balancing act to maintain with trying to stay within budget and to deal with the limited resources and groceries available. Food shortages became an integral component of community life. For me and no doubt for most hard working families, this state of affairs was like an unwanted and undesired personal invitation forced upon every family indiscriminately and without exception. There was no getting away from the shortages no matter how hard one tried.

In most of the shops, queues would form early on in the day at around 8:30am. One had to queue up outside the grocery or butchers if only to obtain the widest choice of availability of foods on offer. Sometimes my mother would come home with only a few items from her shopping list. If you were late joining the queue you could end up with nothing but a pound of dripping!

Mother made the most of mealtimes by spicing things up a little. Mealtimes often then became an adventure to look forward to as the creations served up went from the most bizarre to the basic simple but deliciously delightful spuds with Spam croquette. Friends from school would crash out at our home, especially if they knew that my mother was experimenting with a new dish. She soon became the talk of the neighbourhood but all for the right reasons.

Despite this welcomed glimmer of happiness, the thought of war was never too far away from our minds, especially as we all knew that Daddy had enlisted himself. The time for him to leave us grew ever nearer as his training in Aldershot progressed.

Chapter 3

All Change on the Home Front

A year into the Great War and everything had changed. The landscape looked dark and shell-shocked as the brickwork to many of the prominent and landmark buildings around London lay in ruins having lost its shine in a trade out to the effects of the continuous shelling and bombs unleashed on the capital. In particular, there was a quaint museum on Threadneedle Street which housed shipping memorabilia spanning the last hundred years and which had been dramatically damaged. It was a place much loved by the Harrodians and many others with many patrons enjoying spending Saturday afternoons browsing the corridors of its elegant infrastructure.

It was an impressive building which stood tall and erect albeit a bit musty in places but nevertheless, a place well loved. Now the museum seemed to cower under the burning emblems of the remains of the bombs, its poison oozing from the very core of its existence. Outside on the front door lay a notice which appeared to be singed around the edges. The notice read "closed until further notice and until repair work is completed." Despite the promise of restoring the museum, it was clear that any repair work would be extensive and may be a little over ambitious especially as its once impressive stature now stood forlorn, reduced by the ashes which crumbled around it. The museum had not opened its doors for six months. Surely, the museum had seen better days.

Meanwhile Charles had embarked to the front line to join his comrades and so the house appeared eerily quiet. Not that Charles was noisy but one knew when he was around, perhaps because he smoked a cigar, the aroma of which often filled the entire house. He had however managed to wean himself off the tobacco because Sarah, his wife, had not been too keen for him to continue now that she was expecting.

'I have an interview,' Sarah said approaching Rupert one evening after school.

'Mother.' Rupert exclaimed. 'You cannot go to work, you're needed here and anyway, you're pregnant.'

'It's an interview, not an offer of a job. I may not even get the job,' retorted Sarah. 'I see you do not like the idea of me working but with Daddy on the front line and a baby on the way, we need to make sure everything continues to function as per the status quo. Anyway, it is important that I am seen wherever I can to support the war effort.'

'Well I suppose if you put it that way,' Rupert said, 'it would be an honourable thing to do.'

At this conjecture, George bounded into the room, rosy cheeked and a bit dishevelled from playing rounders with the neighbour's boys. 'Hey,' George said, 'why the glum faces?'

'Oh don't worry your head. Mummy was just talking about going to an interview to secure work.' Rupert replied.

'Work!' exclaimed George loudly.

'Not you as well, George.' Sarah said. 'It seems that you both find the idea of me working preposterous. Anyway, we will see what transpires.'

The weekend came to an end all too soon and the beginning of the school week loomed. Sarah left the boys to tidy up the kitchen and ventured out for a walk and to meet Betsy her friend at the local public house. If she thought being in a different environment might offer some light relief she was mistaken, as thoughts about the war had become all to palpable as the public houses were filled with the elderly and their spouses who had loved ones in the trenches.

'Heard from Charles?' Timothy asked Sarah.

'No, not yet.' Sarah said hurriedly, not wanting to linger on her response too long as she was feeling quite emotional what with George her younger son going through a difficult patch presently, which she had put down to teenage hormones. She was also missing Charles as she had never spent this amount of time away from him. They did everything together and hardly spent any time apart from each other. To the outsider, it would appear that they were in the first stages of love. However, in her mind they were ideally suited and talked about everything together thereby not leaving any room for negativity to fester.

Sarah had agreed to meet her friend Betsy at the local public house. She hardly ventured to the public house as she preferred the comforts of her own home in which she could, as often as she pleased, have a quiet reflective drink. However, she had agreed to go out today as her friend Betsy needed her support. She had therefore offered to accompany her. Betsy's husband had also joined the war effort. He too had worked alongside Charles at the stockbrokers firm but had decided to join his comrades on the battlefield. Betsy had been unable to have children and had miscarried twice. She had subsequently decided that it was too painful to continue trying. Anyway, she was now forty-five and in her mind, a trifle too old to be thinking about having children. The two had bonded over shared interests such as crotchet and knitting and had together sent many a parcel to the front with gifts of woollen hats, mitts and blankets as the soldiers had requested. They were only too glad to help where they could.

'Let's sit over there.' Sarah said, taking the lead and moving deliberately away from the crowd of men who had taken centre stage on the main seating area in the house.

'Yes let's.' replied Betsy. 'I think it's best to speak out of earshot as we don't want to provide any ammunition to the gossip carriers.'

'I suppose we could push the boat out a bit,' Sarah said, 'and order a gin and tonic.'

'I'll second that. We don't often take the opportunity to go out,' Betsy said. Sarah walked up to the serving point and put her order in.

'You sure Charles would approve of you drinking alone. Where's Rupert?' one of the punters shouted out.

Sarah scanned around her to see who had lambasted her. When she saw it was Mr. Toby she decided not to enter into a dialogue with him. It was considered prudent not to do so as Mr. Toby often became inebriated at which point his rhetoric and behaviour could become quite unpredictable.

'That's it - keep that stiff upper lip then.' Mr. Toby retorted. Mr. Toby always seemed to court the wrong kind of attention - a busybody always meddling in other people's business. Gossip had it that he was almost invariably ready for a fight or an argument and it was often said that he wished that people would square up to him so he could show off his skills. He loved to win an argument but Sarah knew better than to rise to the challenge. There was always some busybody trying to organize her life or assume some kind of parental authority for her now that her husband was away. Sarah didn't need mollycoddling. She knew Charles wouldn't care a hoot so long as she didn't get carried away. Assuredly, there was no possibility of that happening; as a respectable wife and pillar of society, she knew her limitations. Sarah walked back to take her seat next to Betsy. The two of them chatted quietly exchanging bits of information about life since their respective husbands had gone off to war. Soon the attention turned to Sarah's children.

'How's George?' Betsy asked.

'I wondered if you were going to broach that topic,' Sarah responded.

Sarah had been troubled for a number of weeks about little George as she fondly referred to him. George had become quite distant and uncommunicative at home. The indicators were that he was spiralling into the first phase of depression. It was becoming quite apparent that the absence of his father, who he was extremely close to, was affecting him immensely.

'George, as you know, is in the first flush of youth and if I had my way, now is not really the ideal time for his father to not be around to provide the stability I think he needs. I have tried everything. His school headmaster is also becoming concerned about him. It is not that he is exhibiting aggressive behaviour but rather that his school work is suffering and his grades have fallen because he neglects to complete his homework. Even his interest in learning the piano has waned somewhat. Charles and I thought he was keen to continue with lessons as he showed such promise.' Sarah continued. 'Charles and I initially thought that Rupert, being the sensitive soul that he is, may suffer more emotionally with his father being away but instead, it would appear that George has come off worse. Rupert has shown himself to be a real trouper.'

'It may be just a phase,' said Betsy.

'How many times have I heard that before,' Sarah said exasperatingly, alarmed at her sharp response. She stopped short and caught her breath. 'Sorry, I didn't mean to sound so abrupt. I just need some clarity as to how to proceed. I have even held off writing to Charles in the hope that George might settle down so that I do not burden him with such sorrowful news. Charles needs moral support right now.' Sarah rattled on.

'I know a young chap, William. His parents live a few doors away from me. He's quite a grounded sort of person and I think he shares some of George's interests. Would you like me to arrange an evening where the two of them can meet up?' Betsy said. 'They are of a similar age group and it would be good for them to talk.'

'Mmmmm, that could possibly work,' Sarah said. 'I will broach the subject delicately with George when I get home.'

Last orders were being called and both Betsy and Sarah decided to have another drink before leaving for home. At precisely 10pm, the punters started to make their way out as the landlord stood at the porch of the door and the punters exited into the cold night air. Sarah's house was only a short walk from the public house and so Betsy parted company with Sarah as it was deemed safe enough for her to make the walk home. Sarah picked up her pace as she walked as the soldiers patrolling the streets hurried people along as the sirens could be heard in the background warning people of an imminent onslaught. Intelligence was usually accurate in this regard and so Sarah needed not to be told twice and managed to open her front door and close it quickly behind her before the attack descended.

The sky turned black as smoke billowed across the night sky showering down pellets and debris from the bomb. Screams could be heard far away as people ran for shelter and to get to where they were going. The hit took place about a mile away from Sarah's home but luckily, she missed the catastrophe. George and Rupert came to the door as Sarah stepped in.

'That was a near miss,' sighed Sarah as George cowered behind the door of the lounge. I'm alright George, all is well, the commotion is much further away than it sounds,' Sarah said, trying to reassure him.

The weekend came to an end all too soon and a new school week beckoned. George had already said he wasn't looking forward to going to school having become quite desperate about the bomb attack which had occurred over the weekend. Sarah had planned to set the alarm an hour earlier so that she and George could have a casual chat before he left for school. George had agreed that this might prove beneficial and so didn't mind losing out on a little bit of sleep. He got up, dressed for school and had breakfast, and after a pep talk, appeared ready to go to school.

George excelled at Geography, English and Science at school but found most of the other subjects challenging. He loved the outdoors though and so the physical education period was something he greatly looked forward to. He had been chosen for the school rugby team and had also recently been nominated to join the inter county rugby team.

The school assembly is an integral component within the school curriculum with everyone gathering for prayers first thing in the morning. In the afternoon, before the end of the school day, each individual class was responsible for organizing their own prayer time before dismissing the class to go home. George found these special times of the day fairly ritualistic but yet comforting.

Morning prayers dispensed with the children shuffled off to their lessons. It was George's favourite day because after lunch his school rugby team would be participating in a friendly match with the Harrow Intercollegiate Rugby Team. George had been selected because of his skills in the Wing Forward position, a position which he had managed to maintain and which had won the school many a trophy. George was excited about the game, not least because it meant not being stuck indoors and having to endure the history lesson which he really hated. His grades reflected his lack of interest in the subject and the thought of playing rugby instead of having to complete the test paper which had been set for today's lesson delighted him.

The bell had gone for lunch and the boys from Year Three headed by Mr. Armitage scrambled to join the orderly queue for lunch. Everyone without exception had to queue up for lunch in an orderly fashion, even the staff, but they queued separately. The school was a stickler for manners and were very rigid in enforcing what was referred to as the 'Code of Conduct.'

No pushing boys,' bellowed Mr. Armitage, 'or you will have to go to the back of the queue.'

With lunch over, the corridors were heaving with children making their way to the first lesson of the afternoon.

'Hey Josh?' shouted out George, it's nearly time, we should be heading to the changing rooms.'

'Oh yeah, almost forgot,' shouted back Josh.

Shouting across the hallway or corridors was frowned upon by the school.

'Quieter please you two, you know the rules, no shouting,' said Mr. Dickson the headmaster, stabbing his finger at the neatly printed notice on the wall.'

'Sorry sir,' the boys said as they picked up their pace. They did not need to be told twice.

As the boys made their way towards the changing rooms they were joined by the rest of the team. They all started to talk very enthusiastically about the game and their tactics for ensuring that their school won the match. Then from a distance a bell could be heard. It was quiet and then it seemed to get louder and louder.

Josh looked around the group. 'Do you hear that noise? Sounds like a bell going off.'

'I can hear something,' Stephen said.

'That's the siren being sounded,' David said

Josh looked around at the group and then at George. 'That's the siren, George. We need to make our way to the patrol area so that we can be marshalled into the bunker.'

'No, that can't be right,' George said.

The siren had never gone off during school hours before but preparations were always in place in the event of a hit . Everyone had been drilled in respect of what to do should the siren sound and refuge in the bunker be deemed necessary. Today was the day when these plans became a reality. The sound of the siren could no longer be masked but its tone was sharp and clear! Along the wooden panelled corridors, classrooms door were flung open as children filed out and made their way towards the bunkers. The boys looked at each other, now no longer in doubt that indeed the siren had been sounded and the realities of the drill of seeking shelter if an incident were ever to occur had become a living reality.

'Fall in line boys,' Mr. Tomkins ordered.

Ashen faced George looked at Josh. Flashbacks of the weekend went off in George's mind. He started running.

'Hey,' bellowed Mr. Tomkins, 'what are you doing. We are never instructed to run but to walk,' he continued.

However, George could not hear or see anyone. In a blind panic he started running even harder and faster but not towards the bunker. George was actually running back home so that he could be with his family. He ran past the patrol area, the bunker, and out of the school gates. Luckily they were open enough for him to squeeze through. He continued running along the streets, darting through other pedestrians who had also been instructed to head towards home if possible or to the public bunkers or underground shelters.

Chapter 4

Family

My mother had written to Daddy and we all added our own little short notes today and included the letter with the parcel that was due to be sent out to him.

'I wonder when it will arrive or even if it will get there?' asked George.

'Of course it will,' Sarah said reassuringly. 'Post out to those in battle are delivered separately,' she continued.

As a family we had taken to writing almost weekly and in return received prompt response letters from Daddy. One such letter read thus:

18 March 1916

Dear family

I have joined the 5th Battalion and I am stationed in Lille, France near the border of Belgium. How is Rupert doing? He's such a sensitive soul. Be strong lad and look after Mother for me. Sarah, say hello to my young son George and hope all is well for the impending birth of the young one.

You asked about trench life but I'd like to spare you the more gruesome details but suffice to say that trench life is rather grim; dark dingy and offering little comfort. I look forward to having a few days away when the baby is born. It will be nice to be back in familiar more comfortable surroundings again. This is a comforting thought.

Some of my comrades haven't fared as well as I have, poor souls. The officers' accommodation offers a little more in the way of comfort but only a smidgen. It is unfortunate that so many have fallen to various illnesses. So perhaps it is advisable that I plan my visit say three months after the baby is born, that way I can be sure that it's safe and less vulnerable. There are lots of rats in the trenches which of course may carry diseases and make you sick. I am much troubled by them disturbing my sleep, if one could but sleep peacefully at all.

You asked about casualties? Unfortunately, there have been a number. I will say improvements are being made to sacredly place fatally wounded soldiers in separate confinement areas as some of my men have had the unfortunate predicament of inadvertently lying side by side with slain bodies. Such has been the intensity of this recent attack that we are behind in schedule in dealing with our fallen comrades. Though it is always sad to see our men fall victim to the enemy, the army chaplains are doing a splendid job. God bless their souls.

How is life in the neighbourhood? It is understood that food shortages are affecting you all but I trust that you are able to manage the budget and that you haven't had to do without. I know it is hard but I hear the war should be over by Christmas and then we can get back to life as it once was.

I long to see you all, and you my sweetheart. I truly hope you are doing fine. It will soon be time to welcome our little newborn into the world, but what a world! And what a time to be born with so much chaos and unsettlement. War is sad but the quiet courage of those around one helps keep one strong. There is a great sense of comradeship that keeps us fighting as we advance forward, our optimism not dimmed, and we remain stoic and resolute as ever to the cause.

We take our lives into our hands every day we are in the front line but I am hopeful I will survive as I must see you again as we have so much to live for.

Keep courage and remember me in your prayers. Hope to see you all soon.

Your father and husband, Charles.

Back at the family home we had just finished breakfast, which was a helping of porridge and bread with homemade raspberry jam. Mother had been fortunate with her shopping list this week and we have fared fairly well with obtaining all that we had written on our weekly shopping list. We cleared up the breakfast plates which was my job that week and sat down to play charades which we often did at the weekend. I had gone out to purchase the daily paper but had put it to one side with the intention of picking it up later once breakfast had been dispensed with.

'George,' Rupert said cheerily, 'pass the newspaper to me.'

'Here,' George said, throwing the paper at him.

'Pass the paper,' Rupert said firmly. George was a bit of a tearaway and Rupert, assuming the role of the surrogate father, tried his hardest to try and tame him and reign his behaviour in.

The headlines bounced off the front page. **It read, "100's hit by shell fire in one fell swoop!"** The headlines jumped out of Wednesday's Guardian. Wednesday 14th July 1916, as if to grab my attention of the realities of war, as if anyone needed a reminder that Britain was at war.

'The savagery of it all!' exclaimed Mother.

The attack had happened at Lille where Father was stationed and our immediate thoughts were to the injured and whether he had been caught up in the exchange of fire. We did not have to wait long to find out as sure enough the next day we received that dreaded knock on the door. At first we thought it was the delivery boy but glancing out of the window I could see two men smartly dressed in dark apparel. We'd seen them before on the other side of the road when our friend's family received the news early that year and now it was our turn. Knock, knock. The noise resounded around the house.

'I'll get that,' said Rupert.

'No, it's alright, I'll get the door,' Sarah responded.

My mother came running down the stairs as I got to the door. She moved ahead of me and opened the door. I stood close to her to offer my support should she need it.

'Mrs. Harrodian?' the officers enquired.

'Yes, I am,' Sarah responded. 'Come in sirs,' she said.

The two men came in carefully wiping their feet on the mat provided. They were smartly dressed in black and one of them carried a brown paper bag in his hand whilst the other man was holding a rather large square brown envelope under his arm.

Mother ushered them into the sitting room. The men sat down and spoke gently with my mother for a few minutes. I didn't want to intrude in on the conversation as I felt Mother needed the privacy so waited for the men to leave. After the debriefing, the two then got up to leave and handed my mother a bag containing my father's personal effects together with some other documents. I was watching my mother from the stairs which provided a view into the sitting room when the door was left ajar. It was clear from her response that something tragic had befallen Daddy. Mother was completely crestfallen. She didn't cry at first. It was if she was holding everything together. However, as soon as the men left, her calm composure gave way to a huge sigh and she let out a scream as if to release the pain of the trauma unfolding before her. Mother crumpled into a heap on the floor.

'Mother,' Rupert cried out as he ran towards her. He enveloped her into a big bear hug with his skinny frame with George following closely, not sure exactly what had happened but sensing that something terrible was amiss. My mother eventually got to her feet, her tear stained face having smudged away her usually flawless complexion.

'George, Rupert, come over and sit down over here,' Mother said. 'I'll put the kettle on,' she continued, trying to sound composed.

'It's alright Mother, allow me.' Rupert said.

With tea made and some homemade bread at the ready, they all sat down huddled together on the sofa trying to comfort one another. Both George and Rupert looking intently at Mother waiting for her to relay what had happened. They didn't want to rush her but needed to hear about the tragedy which had befallen their father. George, being the youngest, didn't quite know what to make of it but seeing his mother upset had made him upset too and he knew that something devastatingly horrid had befallen his father.

'George and Rupert, you know that I have received terrible sad news. I can scarce take it in. We have to be strong for one another,' she continued whilst embracing them close. 'Your father was killed in battle two days ago and the gentlemen you saw leave earlier had come to break the news to me. Your father is very brave no, I mean was very brave. He was killed in service two days ago as his battalion advanced towards the enemy. The officers from the War Office have returned his personal effects,' she said pointing to a brown paper bag which contained her husband's glasses, diary, and a few other personal items. 'They were very kind.'

'How did Daddy die?' little George asked.

'He was, he was...... blown apart by shell fire. His body was found by one of his junior soldiers, Alexander, who had stopped to attend to some of the casualties that had also been slain,' she replied, diverting her eyes away from George and turning to Rupert as she continued. 'The men from the War Office told me that the troops, headed by your father, had been advancing towards the German trench lines to launch an attack and got caught in the crossfire as they were doing so. Apparently, your father had tried to take cover by lying still in the thick mud as the German camp opened fire hoping that the mud might act as a camouflage but he wasn't safe. The remains of a previously fired shell let out its final blast, very much like a smoking gun, and with that, snuffing out any life that remained in him. Poor Charles. Sorry, sorry,' Sarah said, realizing that she may have been a little too graphic in detailing the events of the incident as George had run out of the sitting room screaming, perhaps with the shock of it all and holding his stomach! She realized that she had probably given away too much detail but felt cathartic for doing so as it seemed to help ease the pain of the loss of her beloved Charles.

'Mother,' Rupert said in a comforting tone and placing a strong arm on her shoulder, 'let's not say much more, the details are too shocking to contemplate or even think about.' Rupert then left the room to go and find George. In that moment he realized that so much more was to fall to him in an effort to keep the family together and perhaps be there as a shoulder for the others to cry on. He reflected on the fact that his father would have wanted him to be strong for the family and to share some of the responsibility of making sure that life continued and that George and his mother, and soon to be born sibling, were looked after and supported. A lot therefore was being placed upon his young shoulders.

Chapter Five
Not Coming Home Anymore

The last letters from my father arrived on 16 July and another one on the 12 November and now there were to be no more. The news was slowly sinking in and the reality of knowing that their father would not be coming home again was beginning to dawn upon them all.

'Remember we have lunch with Aunty May today,' Sarah said to the boys as they cleared away the breakfast things. 'I have been thinking Rupert. Now that you are seventeen, perhaps you could enquire about securing work at the munitions factory, after all, George is still young and there is a baby on the way. We have a small pension from the War Office but every additional support is welcome. We do have the house in Cornwall but unfortunately I think it is in need of some repair work. Once this has been completed, we will need to look at selling it.'

A few months had passed since the death of Charles and Sarah was due to give birth very soon. It was to be an autumn birth; Charles' favourite time of the year. Things had become difficult, both emotionally for the Harrodian family and financially too, as women couldn't control their own finances.

So Rupert had taken on the headship of the family being the eldest child and rightful heir.

It was a sunny autumnal day with shades of golden brown leaves strewn over the family home. Sarah had been restless for most of the night so Maureen, the next door neighbour who had become close since the death of Charles, had come round to spend the night with Sarah. Sarah's close friends had presumed that the joy of giving birth to her new baby would perhaps help to heal the pain of losing her husband. However, Sarah had decided that there would be no fanfare or joyous celebration. Instead, the occasion would be marked by a naming ceremony and baby dedication in the usual simple traditional manner and not in any overly glorious fashion.

The vicar, the Right Reverend Richard Donaldson, came to visit the family home a day prior to the baby dedication.

'Hello Reverend Donaldson,' said Sarah as she answered the door, embracing him in a bear hug. This was all she could do to avoid breaking down so publicly and avoid the neighbours vying for front seat viewing. That wouldn't do. Moreover, the birth, though joyous in itself, was tinged with sadness because the date coincided with plans made by Charles before his death. He had planned to take his leave so that he could be at home in time for the birth.

'Hello Reverend and thank you for coming. I very much appreciate you taking the time out of your busy schedule when I am sure you have so many other and more deserving people needing a visit.'

'Come now,' Reverend Donaldson said, 'I am more than happy to visit plus I haven't seen you at church for a while and needed to reassure myself that you and the family were coping with your loss. You do know that we have counsellors on hand who can assist you should you wish to talk through things,' the Reverend continued.

In fact, if truth be told, Sarah had started to attend church services less since the loss of Charles. She had found it hard to regain her faith because she had found it hard to reconcile the loss of Charles with a God of love who she felt had left her without her life partner so that now she was struggling to cope.

'Thank you,' Sarah replied. 'Indeed, I will try to come out more often but as you know, it can be difficult with a newborn in tow.'

Reverend Donaldson simply smiled. 'So remember, the service

starts at 10:30 and we have arranged a small reception in the church hall,' he said with a smile.

Sarah got up to see Revered Donaldson out but he motioned back gently adding, 'not to worry Mrs. Harrodian, I can see myself out. Remember we are here for you,' and with that he closed the door softly behind him.

A few weeks had passed since the baby dedication and with the passing of time, the number of visitors to the Harrodian home became less frequent. A deep gloom, much like a foreboding cloud just before a heavy downpour, had descended on the family as the reality of war and enforced frugality became harder to embrace. Having a child had put pressure on the family resources and in addition, Rachel, their daughter, had become quite a sickly child. No sooner had she recovered from one ailment it was as if another was waiting in the wings.

'Oh dear, oh dear,' sighed Sarah at breakfast.

'What is the matter Mummy, you seem so sad?' George enquired.

'Sad.... Georgie?' Sarah replied 'I don't think sad fully describes my situation at the present. Rachel is a lovely girl, a real sweetie, and we are blessed to have her, but what a drain on our resources. Frankly, I am struggling to cope what with health treatments being so expensive. There are too many mouths to feed.'

'I'll get a paper round job. I'll try to get a job helping at the newsagent, anything.... I want to do my bit.' George ventured.

'No dear, it's alright, you are not quite old enough, we will manage, we will have to manage. I don't want you falling sick like your baby sister.' And so George relented.

Try as she might, nothing seemed to work in curing Rachel. It was the weekend before December and Sarah decided to call a family meeting. She had been able to buy a fruit loaf and some crackers and had arranged a tea using their best china in which to serve it.

'What is the occasion Mother,' Rupert asked.

Well, we may not be able to indulge like this for some time as it is likely that we will have to self impose further food rationing as healthcare for little Rachel is proving frightfully expensive. I want to do everything I can to ensure that Rachel has the best healthcare and this may mean reducing our food shopping or doing without some of our favourite things. For today, I think it would be a lovely idea to have a little tea party to celebrate and remember how things used to be. We can then look back on this day in fondness whenever a sad occasion arises, or if and when we have to make any further sacrifices with regard to Rachel's healthcare. I hope you understand. It should only be temporary because the war should end soon and perhaps Rupert would have qualified by then and we can start living life again. That's it boys, that's all I wanted to say. I don't need you to respond yet. Let's tuck in and enjoy.'

A while after, Rupert stood up. 'Mummy,' he said, 'I will put all my wages to help with the family budget in the hope that the financial pressures can be somewhat alleviated.' By this time, Rupert was twenty-one and he had become a medic in the army on his way to becoming qualified as a doctor and so he was doing his bit for the British Army by helping to treat the wounded. Thankfully he was not serving on the front line but had agreed to become a medic instead as he didn't want the trauma of his mother losing another to the war. Although he was away from home an awful lot, he had managed to arrange time off so that he could help out at home especially now that his mother had her hands full with looking after his younger brother and baby sister.

It was December 20^{th,} five days before Christmas. For the Harrodian family, Christmas was usually a lavish affair with all the family gathering together at their home in Cornwall. But this year, 1919, although the war had ended, Rachel had had pneumonia for the third time and this time the doctors held out little hope for her recovery. Things looked very gloomy indeed and Sarah had on one occasion summoned Reverend Donaldson to the family home to prepare for the last moments with Rachel because she had become so sick; surely, death couldn't be that far away. Reverend Donaldson had suggested that the Harrodians celebrate Christmas with Rachel despite her being terribly poorly in the event that this turned out to be her very last Christmas.

Sarah had been tending to Rachel who had become quite pale and limp. Her once bright blue eyes were shrouded by the dark entrenched circles under her eyelids and her once smooth porcelain skin had become pale and sallow with the constant treatments. Sarah looked down over her child and wept. 'Jesus,' she whispered, 'if she isn't going to get any better then please just take her.... I cannot bear to see her so poorly.' Sarah hardly ever engaged in prayer, but this was more of an earnest plea. 'If you are there Lord Jesus, please end her suffering.' Sarah pleaded. Rupert popped his head around the door. He had heard the quiet sobs and had quietly come to see what was wrong. He placed an arm around his mother's shoulders. He truly loved his sister as she had been so longed for after his mother had miscarried twice whilst carrying girls and therefore understood her grief.

'I heard you praying and I understand your grief Mummy.' He spoke quietly and with gentleness in his voice. 'But could we not try and see what else can be done to help. I have been doing some research and have read about a new treatment that is available in Sweden. Surely we could raise the money and send Rachel for treatment. What do you think?'

'I don't know if we have time on our side,' Sarah replied. 'Rachel looks so weak and she could go at any time.'

'Mummy, don't say that. I couldn't bear the thought of losing her, not now, and so soon after Daddy. We have to be hopeful. I will try to be hopeful for us all.'

'I am trying to be hopeful son, but I just don't know anymore, nothing seems to be working,' Sarah whispered.

The family had gathered at the house in Windsor for Christmas morning. Isabella, Sarah's sister-in-law, had tastefully decorated the home with pretty pink baubles and streams of Christmassy ribbons in colours of orange, pink and cream, hanging from the dado rails. A large tree stood in the hallway, which had been decorated and a fairy placed on top. There were also many Christmas cards from family and well-wishers scattered on the mantelpiece. Rachel loved Christmas and so special attention had been given to the decorations since it could be her last Christmas. Rachel had been propped up on a chair so she wouldn't miss out on the fun. Thoughtful Karen, Sarah's sister, had taken over the proceedings with regard to looking after the guests and organizing the serving of the food. She also made sure that Sarah was free from the cares of looking after Rachel, a job which she assigned to her other sister, Susan.

'Make sure you let me know if I'm needed,' Sarah said to Susan. 'If Rachel needs me, please, I need to be there.'

'Okay, don't worry Sarah, but try and just enjoy this moment and the respite afforded to you, just for today if at all possible,' Susan said kindly.

Dinner was served and the family tucked in. The table was bursting at the seams with roasted potatoes decorated with thyme and rosemary, a whole turkey with stuffing spilling over onto the dish on which the bird lay, and an array of carved meats stood to attention on one side ready for devouring. The flavours, so aromatic, wafted in the atmosphere; who could resist such a meal. They had done really well. No-one would have thought that the war had just ended! Susan gently mashed up some of the food into a paste-like consistency and attempted to feed Rachel, taking her to a more comfortable spot on the chaise lounge. After what seemed like ages, she rejoined the rest of the family at the table.

A game of charades was in full swing. The guests were drinking glasses of port with soda drinks for the youngsters. Everyone appeared to have forgotten the misery that was before them and with Rachel quietly sleeping, or so they thought, Susan felt free to leave Rachel in the side room on the bed to re-engage with the merriment of the evening's celebrations. Sarah joined in too, thankful that most of the family had been able to join her for Christmas despite the heavy snow that had fallen. Sleeping arrangements had been made should it prove too difficult for anyone to return home.

After a while, Sarah popped in to take a look at Rachel who appeared to be sleeping. She then looked more closely only to find that Rachel had quietly slipped away into a deep sleep. Her breathing became more laboured before quietly coming to a stop. Sarah picked up Rachel and placed her on her lap. She sat there stroking Rachel's hair.

Sarah had been gone a while so Rupert and Susan popped their head around to see if all was well. The look on Sarah's face said it all. 'She's gone,' she whispered. 'Her pain is over and she is now at rest.'

'Oh God.............why?' Rupert exclaimed, trying hard to hold back his grief. He stood there numb, still almost. He looked briefly across at his mother and then with his head bowed down low, covered his eyes with his hands and wept silently. 'Rachel, Rachel,' he whispered repeatedly through his sniffles as if trying to rouse her from her slumber. 'Rachel, my sweet sister.'

By this time George and the rest of the family had realized that something was amiss and had joined them at the doorway. Karen suggested that the doctor be called whilst John, her husband, telephoned Reverend Donaldson.

Chapter Six

The End and a New Beginning

It was well documented that Rachel had been terribly sick with pneumonia and with three mouths to feed little money and medical bills, things had become frightfully difficult but nothing could have prepared the Harrodians for another tragedy so soon after losing Charles. Rupert, who had assumed the role of provider, family shepherd and big brother to little Georgie and all round helper, had tried to bring some kind of closure and meaning to the recent chain of events. However, with Rachel passing and his father, nothing he tried had succeeded in bringing her out of her mourning mode. Rupert was also very distraught, but it wouldn't do any good for him to collapse and cave in emotionally though at times he felt he could; he had to assume a stiff upper lip and continue on, stoic and ready to handle anything life dared to throw at him.

In the good old days, the Harrodians, with foresight, had invested heavily in Rupert's education recognizing that he had the potential to do well. Rupert had expressed sincere intentions to become a doctor and so his parents had carefully put some money away so that Rupert's school fees could be taken care of when the time came. However, things proved challenging. With Rachel very poorly, discussions were had in relation as to whether the educational fund for Rupert should be suspended and the monies used to pay for more expensive health treatment for Rachel. The discussion often spilled over into little heated arguments and was often a sore point within the nucleus of the family, as there was a real need to ensure that Rachel had the best possible chances of surviving but also at the same time secure a future for Rupert should the inevitable happen. In the end, fate decided and Rachel passed before any concrete decisions could be made to the contrary.

Prior to Rachel's passing, Rupert had signed up to the army in the capacity as a medic on route to qualifying as a doctor. There was no time like the present to take some time out before qualifying as a doctor to gain some experience treating the wounded at war. Moreover, he needed time away to himself to reflect and try to assimilate the pieces of his stretched emotions. War would toughen him up or so he thought and make him into a stronger person.

'I have enlisted to support the wounded on the front line,' Rupert told his mother.

'But this will mean you will be away from the family,' Sarah said, alarmed at the thought of not having Rupert around to help her out. She had come to rely on him terribly; he was so helpful, super efficient and calming, much like Charles. Rupert had been given the option of deciding whether he wanted to join the army on the account that his father had passed away and that he had assumed the role of head of the family. So Sarah was questioning why he had decided to enlist.

'Mother,' Rupert said, 'I need to acquire as much experience as possible as it will assist me in the long term when I qualify and start looking for work.'

'Ok,' Sarah said with a heavy sigh wishing she could somehow stop him from going away. She needed Rupert at home. Nevertheless, Sarah agreed reluctantly but wished he didn't have to as she had her hands full what with Georgie and Rachel and life in general. She sobered herself with the thought that a few years from now, life would pick up as Rupert took on his first job post qualifying.

'Anyway, I forgot to add,' Rupert said, 'the Chief of Staff at my regiment has agreed to allow me to have every weekend off and work only a four day week if I wish to. This should ensure that I am around at the weekends to help out where you need me to,' he said.

'But then it is not worth you really going Rupert if you are only working a four day week,' Sarah said. 'You might as well work the whole week and come home every other weekend.'

'We'll sort something out,' Rupert replied, not quite sure of how it was going to all work out. 'If it doesn't work out Mother, I will just draw a line under it and come home,' Rupert said consolingly.

Monday 16ᵗʰ September. On a bright sunny spring morning, Rupert prepared to leave for Southampton. He had been up most of the night packing but also trying to resolve the lingering thoughts of whether he should still continue with his plans.

'Do you really need to go,' Sarah said to Rupert tearfully, tugging at his arm in a last minute attempt to persuade him not to go. 'I've got my hands so full I'm not sure if I can cope,' she continued.

'Mother...,' Rupert said soothingly, 'I promise I will come straight home if my absence proves too much of a burden to you, really I will,' Rupert reassured. 'Right, that's me ready,' he said. 'I'll see you soon. I promise it won't be long.' And with that, Rupert had closed the door behind him as he made his way to the station to meet up with the other soldiers who were travelling down that day.

Home for Rupert during the week at least would be the dilapidated medical shack on the dirt track behind the tents, which served as the sleeping quarters of Regiment 5 Hooton. Apart from the location of the Medical Unit, everything else around contained within was sterile or as sterile as could be given the circumstances. As time moved on, Rupert was beginning to find it increasingly difficult to deal with the traumas of war as he struggled to understand the reasons for the war. He was gravely impacted by the daily tasks of dealing with various atrocities. In particular, shrapnel wounds, which would leave the skin badly burned causing one to bleed profusely and ooze with puss. Furthermore, having to handle one-limbed bodied personnel, and disembodied heads, like the walking dead. But somehow Rupert was buoyed on by the principle that if one could save a life then one's job was to do just that irrespective of the perceived quality of life. For Rupert, the central focus was being postured to help to maintain the family unit by treating the wounded soldiers so they were able to go back to their respective families even if they were not completely whole. However, there were some who couldn't be rescued, restored, or patched up, and this Rupert found hard to deal with.

Being amongst the wounded on the front line provided Rupert with a constant daily reminder of his father and the tragedy which befell him. Rupert longed for home. Rupert so badly wanted to return home but deferred from doing so until his transitional period was complete; this being a three-month assignment. Indeed, that day couldn't come soon enough.

The dawn sun rose in the blue sky. Summer was here. Pretty lilac blossoms littered the streets. Soon Rupert would be home. He should be happy but instead his mind was filled with morbid thoughts about his experiences. How could one ever justify war Rupert mused within himself?

Rupert stood outside the front door of the family home looking around to see if anything had changed. He hesitated, and then he rang the bell. His mother was expecting him as he had written to her just a few weeks ago to let her know he was coming home. He heard the patter of feet quickly walking towards the door. The door flung open. Sarah flung her arms around Rupert.

'Rupert, Rupert my boy, let me take a look at you,' Sarah said. 'You appear to have lost a little weight but you look well my boy, indeed, army life suits you,' Sarah teased.

Rupert enveloped both his mother and George in bear hugs. 'Lovely to see you both – home finally,' said Rupert letting out a heavy sigh. 'Hello Mother,' he said solemnly, closing the door behind him whilst sniffing up the aroma of cooking coming from the kitchen. 'Mmmmm, something smells good.'

'I've cooked your favourite. Lamb roast with lots of gravy,' Sarah said.

'Wow, gosh, thank you. How did you manage to get lamb?' Rupert queried.

'Never you mind boy,' Sarah teased. 'Nothing is too good for my boy,' she exclaimed. 'You appear a little sad,' Sarah said, trying to read him as she stood there looking into his eyes.

'The ravages of war.......... it is terrible, terrible,' Rupert exclaimed. 'I don't think I will be going back,' he said softly.

'What did you say,' Sarah said, straining her ears as by this time she had hurried back to the kitchen to finish off the cooking.

'I'm not going back to the front,' Rupert said loudly but

decisively not really wishing to speak about his experiences but more to let his mother know she would get her wish after all.

'Why? You can tell me all about your experiences after dinner, she volunteered. Nonetheless, despite the concern in Sarah's voice, the fact that Rupert was not going back was indeed music to her ears.

Despite the unforgettable experience of treating the walking dead, as was the common phrase at the medical camp, Rupert believed he was now ready for a new challenge and had just twenty-four months before he would have completed his medical training. However, Rupert's mood remained disturbed and overshadowed by the morbidity of the war. But to Rupert, he had done his best as a medic on the front line and in supporting the war effort, giving back to society much needed support to the brave men who volunteered for war not knowing whether they would be returning home to their families.

Chapter Seven

The Prankston Family

It is August 15th on a bright Wednesday morning and Caroline Prankston is due to give birth within two weeks or so as advised by her midwife Valerie.

Ding-dong. The doorbell sounded down the hallway. Ding-dong. Caroline slowly made her way to the front door calling out for her husband but there was no reply as he had gone out on errands. Caroline opened the door to see Katy her friend standing there with some flowers.

'Hello Caroline, these are for you,' Katy said.

'Thank you,' Caroline said.

'Gosh, you look ghastly white and pale this morning, are you alright?' Katy asked.

'Oh dearie me, I have been having pains and I think I may be in the early stages of labour,' Caroline said.

'But you're not due for another two weeks!' Katy exclaimed.

'Oooooooh!' Caroline screamed, puffing out with all her might as if her cheeks would blow up any minute now! She was clearly in a lot of pain.

'I think you should sit down,' said Katy 'and I will call for an ambulance,' she continued.

'Don't trouble yourself,' Caroline said. 'I don't think I am quite ready to give birth yet,' she whispered calmly.

'Let the doctors decide. You look like you need to be in their care,' said Katy in a matter of fact manner.

'Okay,' Caroline replied weakly, not having any more strength to put up a fight.

Katy telephoned for an ambulance and one arrived in four minutes. 'Thank God you got here quickly,' she said as she opened the door to let the medics in.

'You were lucky. We were just finishing attending to a person four streets away when your call came through. They quickly set up the monitoring equipment and ushered Caroline into the ambulance.

"I will get a taxi and meet you at the hospital,' Katy said. 'Don't worry Caroline, I will get there as quickly as possible.' Caroline nodded her head in agreement.

'Don't you worry Mrs. Prankston,' the medic said, 'we will get you to the hospital as soon as possible.'

The siren could be heard as the ambulance whizzed through the streets to the hospital. Arriving at the hospital, Caroline was ushered by Daphne Boxall, the Matron, into the treatment room. 'Who do we have here,' asked Matron.

'Mrs. Caroline Prankston of 42, Blossom Vineyard. 23rd June 1890. We believe she is in the first stages of labour,' replied the paramedic.

By this time, Caroline was writhing in pain and her gasps for air could be heard quietly as she struggled with birthing pains. The staff were summoned and quickly moved into their places as they proceeded to attend to Caroline wheeling her into the side room that had now been prepared.

'Gas please,' shouted one of the doctors to the midwife. Analeese, who by now had heard that her friend Caroline was in labour, came into the room to assist. White-coated men and starched uniformed nursing personnel scurried around Caroline in a rushed fashion as the stern faces on the doctors present peered over assisting with the more complex matters of the birth. It was clear that she was much further gone into labour than initially diagnosed. Moreover, from the hushed tones of the doctors who had been summoned into the room, it was clear that there was some urgency to ensuring that the baby was delivered as quickly as possible. Meanwhile, Analeese who came alongside her to assist with the breathing techniques was comforting Caroline.

'Small breaths,' she said softly. 'Breathe.....................'
'Breathe.....................' 'Now pant, pant, pant,' Analeese encouraged.

Dr. Rupert took his position and seemed to struggle with the task given to him. He appeared to struggle with maintaining the vital signs of both mother and baby and this was causing great stress to Caroline. Meanwhile, due to the passage of time, the senior doctor decided to proceed to deliver the baby by forceps. After what appeared hours, Caroline gave birth to a boy whom she went on to name Thomas.

It would be a week before Caroline was allowed to go home as she had suffered complications at birth and it was considered prudent that she spent time in hospital recovering. On his usual rounds, Caroline was to be seen by the senior doctor on duty that day, Dr. Andrews, who had come in with his team including Dr. Rupert.

'Hello Mrs. Prankston, how are you? We are happy for you to go home today. Do you feel well enough to go home?' the doctor asked.

'Yes I am, and would like to go home today and not a day later,' Caroline replied promptly trying to sound as perky as possible although she still felt a bit weak. It was clear that Caroline did not like hospitals as she had made such a fuss at being kept in for so long after she had given birth. However, she understood and had submitted to the medical team's better judgment. She had been told that the team had experienced some difficulty with the birth but had not been given a full account of the events. The upshot of the situation was that her child, whom she was to name Thomas, was born with a severe lung deformity. The family had been informed that his lung deformity might affect his quality of life.

Subsequently, Thomas suffered terribly with flu, asthmatic

episodes and intermittent epilepsy and the Prankston family were finding it a struggle to meet the financial commitments which come with a sick child.

During the birth, Dr. Rupert had been called upon to support the team who had been assigned to Caroline upon admission. He had recently qualified and his experience on the front line during the war had been well documented. However, he had a penchant for obstetrics and was pleased that he had secured a post at the Pendlebury Hospital.

Something had gone wrong in the delivery room for sure and an investigation was to follow. Furthermore, with recent developments surrounding the procedural aspects of the birth, it was expected that Dr. Rupert's assistance would be called into question.

Chapter Eight
A Fallen Hero

There had been a hive of activity in the birthing room and Dr. Rupert had seemingly caused a stir but for the wrong reasons. With all the commotion surrounding the preliminary investigations of the incident regarding Thomas Prankston, Dr. Rupert had taken himself away from the place of his medical training and had taken up a medical post in Cambridge. Some believed he had retreated to lick his wounds. Only Rupert himself knew why it was important for him to be away from the neighing crowd. He had always loved Cambridge with its landscape and architecture and above all, he wasn't known there. He could quietly get on with life without the prospect of dreading reading anything adverse that some scurrilous or unscrupulous journalist may think prudent to write about him. Since the incident, the press had given him an awful time and this was probably due in part to his family connections. His mother had despaired about him moving so far away from the family home but he thought it was for the best. However, Rupert went to London regularly to be with his mother. He had very dark days and the only thing that would help sometimes would be to spend time with his mother. Although his mother provided much needed emotional support, Rupert often wished that his father was still around. He would know how to fix things and the right words to say.

Rupert had completed his final training at Cambridge University on an exchange programme and before graduating had been offered an internship at one of the leading hospitals in the city of Cambridge. At the time, he had discussed the options with his mother but had decided to return to London so that he could be on hand to support his mother and be around for his younger brother.

Meanwhile, investigations regarding the medical incident on Thomas, Mrs. Prankston's child, had begun. Dr. Rupert had cause to visit Pendlebury Hospital as he had secured some private work in the private unit at the hospital where he specialized in general medicine. It was good in one way that he was around as he was in an ideal position to gauge the opinions of his fellow professionals and perhaps gain some much needed support. However, for some of his colleagues, it sometimes proved that being at the hospital meant he was too near the scene of the incident if you like and was often not a very pleasant person to be around. The finger of blame was being pointed directly at Dr. Rupert and his family had become the scourge of the town. He would snap very quickly and could become quite irritable, even unintentionally. I suppose it was a heavy burden to carry coupled with the fact that this isolated lack of judgment could spell the end of his career.

It was hard, very hard to go out, even to pick up a few items at the grocery store without people whispering and wagging their fingers. 'Oh the shame of it,' exclaimed Sarah.

This was not the clean start and break that Rupert had envisaged or even hoped for. Everything had started out so well. It had been a while now since he had returned to the mainland and accepted a position at Pendlebury Hospital in Kensington and had secured a place in the Obstetrics Department. I suppose this was cathartic and a welcome change for him as it meant as a doctor he would be responsible for bringing new life into the world, a contrast to presiding over so many deaths and bloody conditions the war had offered up to this point. Nevertheless, the accusations wouldn't stop and it looked like the Prankston family were not in a mood to reconcile and patch things up without a thorough investigation.

Dr. Rupert had sought the advice of senior medics in the profession and those who he had befriended at Pendlebury. He had also been given the opportunity to look at the complaint being made against him. Analeese, the midwife, who worked alongside him on the day, had provided her account of the day's events. The chain of events provided by Analeese provided a chance for Dr. Rupert to consider his defence and counterstatement.

Thomas, Mrs. Prankston's son, had agreed to support his mother in her investigation and was therefore very keen to gather the facts as clearly as they could be recalled. He had on a number of occasions visited Analeese who in turn had happily volunteered information as she had a vested interest in Caroline having been a close friend for over ten years.

'Friday 12th of June,' Analeese had said. 'I remember the day so well as if it had been yesterday,' Analeese reflected when she agreed to meet Thomas for lunch to talk over the events of the day almost twenty-one years ago. It wasn't as if the events hadn't been revisited countless times with Thomas having the full knowledge that his mother had on numerous occasions rehearsed the day's events. However, it was a pivotal time for the family and for Thomas equally because he needed closure primarily because he knew his mother was still traumatized by what had happened.

'When your mother had finally been admitted to hospital, the contractions becoming more rapid. It was clear that she was definitely in labour. Because of the way the baby was positioned the medical team had to use forceps to help with your arrival into the world. You were literally born with the umbilical cord around your neck like a metallic choker. Dr. Rupert was the second most senior practitioner on the team and present at the birth and he was supported by two other more junior doctors with the consultant Derek Andrews having ultimate responsibility. We could see the position you were in and it was quite apparent that quick action was needed if you were to survive.' Thomas just listened. He didn't like to interrupt but wanted to make sure he got all the facts or as much as Analeese could recall. Analeese continued.

'Dr. Rupert appeared to be distracted with dealing with the other elements surrounding your mother including fiddling with the blood pressure monitor and the breathing apparatus which is something normally attended to by the junior doctors. It seemed ages before he realized that the baby was in difficulties amidst the obvious fact that the junior doctors were struggling with the forceps. Your head was already out at this point and it was clear that the umbilical cord was around your neck and you were turning blue with each twist and turn of the forceps. The other two doctors signalled to Dr. Rupert that his intervention was required but it was as if he didn't hear them or seem to feel the urgency of the situation as he just continued to do what he was doing. Then it was about two minutes later and one of other doctors shouted out to him, I think it was Dr. Winsome. "Dr. Rupert, I think we're losing him, the baby is becoming limp, unresponsive physically, and bluer." At this point Dr. Rupert turned around, his eyes seemed glassed over, and he quickly came over, unwound the cord from around your neck, passed the baby to the Sister muttering something about taking it through to the Neonatal Unit and proceeded to continue with dealing with your mother. At this point, the consultant Derek Andrews stepped back into the room. He had been called away to attend to an emergency.

'Where were you whilst all this was going on,' asked Thomas.

'I was attending to your mother and trying to keep her as comfortable as possible. I didn't want the stress of the situation that was clearly evolving to affect her any more than it had already.' Analeese said.

'Why didn't you intervene if you sensed danger?' Thomas asked Analeese.

Analeese paused for a moment and then carefully scripted her response. 'Dr. Rupert was a person who commanded authority and didn't embrace counsel, good or bad. He wasn't really an approachable person. He just gave orders and they were meant to be obeyed. Rarely did anyone ever challenge him without being dressed-down publicly, probably as a deterrent to anyone else who dared to challenge or criticize him.'

Thomas was quite satisfied that Analeese had clarity of the events of that day and considered her recall of events to be accurate. However, to him, the whole event was avoidable and could have been prevented! Thomas reflected on this fact and concluded that the outcome could have been very different otherwise.

The hearing had been set for April and there was a lot to do to prepare for the hearing. Additional statements had to be prepared in addition to those already provided. The victim's family had to prepare themselves mentally and for Thomas, upon whom the attention was largely focused, it was difficult. The details of that fateful day had not been heard of or exposed before. It was therefore news worth reporting on and the media pack were in a frenzy. They were out to get a story at any cost.

The Harrodians were held in high esteem so it was difficult for those of them who knew them to take sides. A good proportion of the community stayed loyal to the family and therefore shied away from giving formal interviews to the press even if in support of Dr. Rupert. It was reassuring for the Harrodian family to know that the support was there for them despite the fact that it was not publicly apparent. For the most part, it was generally understood by the general public that medical mistakes could be made and that Dr. Rupert should not be made a scapegoat as there were many who could testify to his capabilities and soothing bedside manner. What mattered to them were the reasons why it happened and what could be done for the family in providing support for Thomas. This was for the tribunal to decide.

'Thankfully the Prankstons are not a vindictive lot,' Dr. Rupert said, 'otherwise they would be taking out a civil claim against me and surely that would finish me off.' They were not close friends though but friendly enough and polite even before the incident.

Obviously, they had been advised by their legal team to distance themselves from the Harrodians during the hearing but this did not stop the press hankering after a story or plugging into any salacious gossip. But thankfully, both families were too sensible to follow that route. Before and up to the days before the tribunal hearing and the days that followed, Dr. Rupert's usual calm and seemingly unruffled exterior had been replaced with doom and foreboding; what with accusations flying around concerning rumours of sabotage, professional inefficiency, and insubordination.

A chorus of voices rang out as news that the tribunal proceedings had started. It was to be a fairly protracted process, about three months the Harrodians were advised so as to allow for due process and all parties involved in the hearing to be called. Both parties in the case were advised that a conclusion might not be ready for at least nine months to a year. The proceedings were proving to be really taxing for Dr. Rupert as his work was being scrutinized daily and with the pressure of the tribunal's decision looming, Dr. Rupert was feeling extremely stressed. At home with his mother, Sarah, Rupert was looking all forlorn and quite pale.

'You need a holiday, that's what you need,' his mother said.

'What now!' Rupert replied. 'I can't. I've got a trial to prepare for and I don't want to be far away from the area. I think it is best to get stuck in, that way I don't have time to brood over what might happen......' Rupert said quietly.

'I see what you mean,' Sarah said, 'but I hate to see you like this looking so sad.'

'Well not long to go,' Rupert said, trying to sound positive. But no matter how he tried to stay positive it was difficult not to think of the worst possible outcome; the end of his medical career, and all that hard work for nothing. And, oh the shame if the community ostracized him should there be a guilty verdict.

As if his mother could read his mind, Sarah said out loud, 'but it might never come to that.'

'Mother, you always know what I'm thinking. Nothing has changed there then.' Rupert said fondly. How reassuring to know that his mother was as intuitive as ever. He had had to look to her for support for everything after his father had died. She had done well in keeping the family together. What would have we done without her? Rupert considered within himself.

Chapter Nine

The Verdict

Rupert arrived at court flanked by his mother and younger brother George and his close medical colleague who had qualified and worked alongside him. Other supporting family friends had joined him to provide moral support. Rupert had placed his solace, faith, and hope in a judicial medical tribunal system finding in his favour and that at the heart of the matter he was not a maligned person, but rather a person in need of emotional support and help. Everything, especially his career, hinged on him being found not guilty and being granted the opportunity to continue his medical career. He prayed and hoped that the outcome would be favourable. He didn't have long to wait.

Men dressed in grey suits huddled together outside the courtroom before the parties were allowed in. The parties were ushered into the room and shown to their seats. Rupert sat with his family with his legal team to the left of him.

Ten minutes to go and Rupert would know his fate. He pondered deeply within himself. Where were all those who had clamoured to work alongside him? They were nowhere to be seen now. It appeared that they had deserted him. At least he had been able to muster some support in gathering opinion from expert witnesses who were able to prove a causal link between emotional trauma and stress and the impact which it could have on one's work. All he needed now was the evidence to be given the weight it deserved and a decision made, which would enable him to continue practicing as a doctor, a job which he loved immensely.

The tribunal session started promptly at 10:30 and the panel summarized their findings and retired to consider their verdict. This was the final stage as witnesses, expert opinions, and various consultations, some public, but some done in private, had all been aired. It had been a lengthy case; 144 days in total as expert witnesses had been brought in. It appeared that everyone wanted a piece of the action, unsurprisingly so, as this was the first case of its kind and as such brought a lot of attention from the media and many other public bodies.

The panel entered the room with its green benches aligning the right side of the room. The panel consisted of Dr. Charles Fitzroy Stevens-Moggs for the General Medical Counsel, court staff, Presiding Chair for the Medical Tribunal, Mr. Pilkington, and a number of persons from the Compliance Board from the hospital where the incident had taken place. On the other side of the room were Dr. Rupert's team together with Dr. Rupert and friends of the family. They stood as the panel entered and were then asked to take their seats. The Tribunal Chair, Mr. Pilkington, began to address the panel and the other attendees at the hearing. The room fell quiet as Mr. Pilkington read through the dossier and began to firstly summarize the findings and then to deliver the decisions made by the panel.

The Truth Comes to Light.
The Tribunal Ruling, Cause, and Effect.

The medical tribunal has established the existence of cause and effect, the root of which lay in the emotional trauma Dr. Rupert had suffered not once, but twice; this being the death of his father and the death also of his baby sister. It is therefore determined that there is the absence of modus operandi and there was no motive or preconceived plan which could be construed as wilful negligence. It also transpires from the investigations that Dr. Rupert at the time was suffering with post traumatic war distress having witnessed the most harrowing atrocities and fallout of the Great War. He had however managed to keep this hidden from those he worked with so that no one really suspected how deeply he had been impacted.

Every killer has his own method of attack; it usually involves a maligned process upon which a criminal investigation would be based. In the case of Dr. Rupert, there is no such criminal activity to investigate.

The decision has been made to arrange to link Dr. Rupert with a counsellor so that he can receive clinical and pastoral counselling.

Rupert sat with his eyes closed tight in an attempt to avoid hearing anything unpleasant. But then he sat up with a jolt as he heard the words 'free to continue his career but with supervision.'

'Thank God,' exclaimed Rupert. 'There is a God somewhere!' he continued. Then realizing that all eyes were on him, Rupert set about sheepishly steadying his composure. 'So sorry,' he muttered. But really, he was so elated! Who cares about the supervision, he mused within himself, at least I have my profession and the opportunity to restore my dignity. I mustn't cry or act up emotionally, Rupert thought within himself – wait until the session is dismissed.

The upshot of the decision was that Dr. Rupert would be given the opportunity to continue his career but was to be placed on probation with supervision for twelve months. Mitigating for Dr. Rupert, his counsel had argued that the panel should recognize the fact that Dr. Rupert had suffered emotionally since the passing of his father and it was this fact coupled with the post traumatic stress of treating the wounded soldiers that perhaps contributed to the lapse of judgment on the fateful day. The Chair of the Tribunal agreed with the direction of Dr. Rupert's counsel and softened the blow by saying that there should be a period of counselling together with a period of supervision. Counselling would commence forthwith.

The caveat to the tribunal decision was that Dr. Rupert would only be able to resume independent practice if he could commit wholeheartedly to the Hippocratic Oath, which enshrines and underpins the code of conduct to which all doctors must adhere.

For the Prankston family, the Medical Tribunal awarded the family the princely sum of £50,000 pounds to include an additional ex gratia payment of £3,000 pounds. This money would be used for medical expenses and the balance to be held in trust until Thomas became of age.

The matter was closed, decision executed, chapter completed. Closure. Five years of hell and uncertainty had drained Rupert and brought upon him a state of anxiety. Rupert had suffered. Some would say that it was no more than he deserved but today their thoughts and comments no longer mattered. All that mattered was that he was free to continue doing the job he loved. His family had supported him throughout and his mother in particular had been a tower of strength for him.

Exit centre stage. The Harrodian family stop briefly to speak with their legal team and to thank them for their support throughout.

'It was a good outcome, perhaps more than what we expected,' a member of Rupert's legal team motioned.

'Indeed,' Rupert agreed, smiling weakly.

Mrs. Prankston and Thomas both ventured towards Rupert and extended their hands towards him to greet him. Rupert hesitated at first. He looked across at his mother and she smiled at him encouragingly, intimating that he should be gracious in receiving their gesture. Rupert extended his hand and shook the hands of both Thomas and his mother firmly.

'Sorry,' he said quietly.

'It's over,' Caroline said. 'We do not bear any grudges. A new chapter can now begin,' she finished.

With pleasantries over, both families walked towards the door to make their exit. The court ushers, quickening their steps, rushed ahead of them to open the doors in an attempt to try and usher the parties quietly out of the building. Unfortunately, as soon as the doors parted, the media scrums were waiting for them like a pack of lions.

'I suppose they expected to see tears and grave faces,' Sarah said.

'You bet,' replied Rupert, his heart a lot lighter than when he first arrived.

It would seem though that counsel for both parties had been advised to be as nonchalant as possible as they exited and to give nothing away if just to avoid any scurrilous reports being written by the press. They were also advised to say little or nothing personally, and to leave it to their respective spokespersons to speak to the press if they saw fit.

The families tried to navigate their way down the steps to access the waiting cars parked outside.

'What a circus,' lamented Sarah. 'Why can't they leave us alone?

They'll get their story no doubt, but they need to know when to quit,' she continued.

Ironically, the infamy of being hounded for a medical error is not one which Rupert thought would grace his CV or feature in the illustrious medical career he had planned. Nevertheless, he was determined that although this incident may appear to many to be a fall from grace, he had decided that he would use it as a stepping stone to help him to become a better doctor and thereby eventually take the sting out of the trauma and the experience of the past months.

Chapter 10

A Journey of Travail

It is December 31st 1923, one of the coldest days on record Rupert noted. It had snowed heavily for two weeks straight and he had been busy every day clearing a footpath from the gate of his home allowing his mother and younger brother to be able to navigate their way out should they need to go out. At least for now though the snow showers had abated.

The war had been over for a while but England was still a sad place with the daily images of the injured returnees from the war who had been signed off as unfit for service. Rupert felt it was important to live as normally as possible and so had agreed to meet up with his friend Peter for coffee. Both had supported the war effort but in different capacities and as they had not met since graduation, there was much to talk about. So coffee was good. They had agreed to meet up to read the papers and discuss plans for a holiday for the forthcoming year.

As they sat at coffee, Rupert reflected on the state of affairs in London. Britain looked so depressed and it's not surprisingly so because of the number of men starting out so valiantly and proud to be representing their country but at the same time oblivious to the horrors of war that lay before them. Many of the young men conscripted into the army had been caught up in patriotic fervour only to return home maimed and disillusioned but also perhaps deepened in spirit and sobered. Many were only too thankful that their fate was not as some of their comrades, some being eviscerated, cut in two, or decapitated. They were though forever traumatized by the horrors of the Great War, united in grief for those who they had left behind, presumed dead on the front line in the trenches and for all those who had given their all in life and death on the battlefield.

Meanwhile, Thomas Prankston had gone on an adventure of his own. Too poorly to sign up, he had spent many a day working out the best way to deal with his physical challenges. He knew that his could have been very different but he had no intention to live his life as a victim forever. He knew the stance his mother had taken and how his disability had overshadowed the enjoyment of a normal family life.

So unbeknownst to his family, Thomas set about planning his own personal quest to locate Dr. Rupert. He had questions that he so badly needed answers to, answers that could only be given by Dr. Rupert.

Thomas knew only too well the emotional trauma he could be opening up for himself but felt that he needed that peace before he could move on with his life fully. His mind was crowded with lots of questions.

'What would be his first reaction when and if he met Dr. Rupert? Would he cry? Would he become emotional, or would be so angry that he would lash out at him?' He knew he held a little resentment in relation to his quality of life and needed to release this. Thomas further hoped that somehow by talking things through with Dr. Rupert, the anger would be redirected appropriately. And so the quest for the truth began in earnest.

Thomas wasn't really interested in the legal or clinical proceedings of the case but was rather keen to learn more about the man behind the role. He had made meticulous plans and implemented a strict code of adherence, or so he called it, within his game plan. It was a three-point plan. Dr. Rupert had to be still living in the UK, agree to contact, and still be practicing as a doctor. If he discovered that Dr. Rupert had moved abroad and did not want to connect with him, he would scupper all searches and lay everything to rest.

Thomas decided to take on the role of spoof. He needed to ascertain whether Dr. Rupert was this monster that people had been saying he was, or whether he had suffered a momentarily lapse of consciousness. He had come across the trial and the media coverage of it at the library and he wanted to carry out his own investigations. Essentially, he wanted to know Dr. Rupert's take on the matter - his side of the story.

In his quest for further knowledge and to gather as much information as possible, Thomas had continued searching and more poignantly, attempted to try and establish a clearer picture of who Dr. Rupert really was. In his search, Thomas had stumbled upon numerous reports and even medical journals written by Dr. Rupert and published by the General Medical Council. Some of this literature contained some impressive testimonials. Thomas had come to the conclusion that perhaps Dr. Rupert was not a bad, mean spirited guy as many had tried to make out and perhaps he been through some trauma of his own and it was perhaps this which had caused him to err and make a number of medical errors. There were numerous glowing reports written about Dr. Rupert, how he tended the sick and wounded on the front line, often going beyond the call of duty. Scores of testimonials had been written about him but he noted how bizarre that none of this had surfaced during the tribunal hearings.

Wednesday morning the 15th [of] June. After weeks of endless searching, Thomas trawled one more time through the cinematic films of the war and micro photographic slides. There were still pictures of soldiers from the Great War in the trenches and some of the heroic medics who were assisting on the field at the time. Thomas was looking for anyone with names either ending or starting with Rupert.

There were lots of names which meant nothing to him. Then he came across a list of medics who had served in the Great War and also those who had lost their lives in the line of duty. Paul Craig, Corporal, Jason Murdock, Lieutenant Commander, Stephen Gall, Flight Lieutenant, Commanding Officer, Rupert Barks, Stephen David Rupert, Charles Slater, Rupert Harrodian. Thomas had been searching archives all day every day, every medical journal he could get his hands on including an assortment of medical bulletins in the hope that something would help him locate where Dr. Rupert was working.

'Whoah.....................,'exclaimed Thomas. 'I found him. I think I have found him.' Thomas exclaimed loudly.

'Shhhhh, you're in the library. We have not come here to read only to have our peace disturbed by you, you loony,' said the man who was quietly reading the Telegraph.

'I do beg your pardon,' Thomas said, forgetting where he was for a moment.

The man looked round as Thomas spoke. He recognized the face from somewhere. 'Thomas Prankston........... Mr. Prankston,' the man said, raising his head ever so slightly to make sure he was not mistaken. 'How you have grown. You look well…and I see, no longer using a wheelchair.'

'We know each other?' quizzed Thomas, taking a second but closer look at the man who stood before him. He stood there for a moment trying to rack his brain as to why he should know this man. And then it dawned on him. 'Mr. Peterson, my old history teacher. I dare say the years have not been too good to you,' Thomas said hesitantly, hoping not to cause offence.

Thomas recalled that Mr. Peterson had sported blond hair which had had a natural wave. He was much liked by the girls, although he recalled he must have been at least in his late forties at the time. He had aged somewhat and being quite tall, had developed a stoop.

'What were you getting excited about earlier?' Mr. Peterson

asked, inquisitively. He gestured further. 'So what brings you here today? Are you not at the office today?'

Thomas hesitated to reply, initially considering whether he should divulge his real reason for visiting the library today. He did not want to give away too much information to avoid sounding silly and to avoid the barrage of questions which undoubtedly would follow. In the end, he decided to chance it.

'Well....' he started off....'now you mention it, I was looking for the whereabouts of a Dr. Rupert. He used to practice in central London about 8 to10 years ago. I was wondering whether Dr. Rupert still practiced medicine and whether he was still around?' Thomas wasn't expecting an answer as he realized that his questions would seem rather random especially to Mr. Peterson for afterall, what did he know about medicine?

'In answer to your question,' Mr. Peterson said hesitantly, 'I believe Dr. Rupert is working at the Pendlebury Hospital in Kensington.

'Kensington; Pendlebury......' the words stumbled out of Thomas' mouth so quickly. 'Really? How do you know?' Thomas asked, quizzing him closely.

'I used to work at the Pendlebury in the laboratory. Your case was big news at the time. It generated a lot of attention both within the hospital and in the media. I followed your case closely all those years ago,' Mr. Peterson said.

Thomas stood still for a moment digesting the information he had just received. Dr. Rupert, alive and still practicing at a hospital only a stone's throw from where I live. His thoughts raced. 'Really,' exclaimed Thomas. 'You mean currently?'

'Indeed,' Mr. Peterson said. 'I tell you no lie. In fact I saw him last week when I visited a friend of mine who is suffering with cancer.'

'Sorry to hear that, I wish your friend a speedy recovery,' Thomas replied.

'Well, I still maintained my contacts at the hospital and indeed, Dr. Rupert has a surgery at the hospital during the week,' Mr. Peterson responded. 'Your case garnered a lot of media attention and people were very interested in the whole saga.'

'Yes, I know,' Thomas said 'so I am told. I was a toddler at the time and much too young to remember or understand anything but my mother speaks of nothing else especially when faced daily with the realities of my difficulties.'

'Yes, very sad,' Mr. Peterson said, nodding.

Mr. Peterson had been his history teacher whilst at school. Since retiring, he often visited the library and it was clear that his love for all things historical had not waned. It was not a known fact that Mr. Peterson had an earlier career as a hospital laboratory technician - a useful nugget no doubt perhaps, Thomas mused within himself.

Fear flooded Thomas's mind as the reality of finally discovering that Dr. Rupert was still alive sunk in. He would get his wish after all to meet with him. Did Mr. Peterson really know of Dr. Rupert's whereabouts? If he did, this was music to his ears. Perhaps now he would be able to put the past behind him. He had carried this burden for so long; the burden being so much heavier to bear because of the impact it had had on his mother. For her, it seemed like only yesterday that the incident happened. Thomas felt that perhaps people did not see him as a real man because he had not served in the Great War. Sometimes Thomas wished he could turn back the clock and start all over but of course, this wasn't possible. That is why it was imperative to him, as much as it was to his mother, to bring some kind of closure to it all.

Chapter Eleven
Restoration and Forgiveness

After the trial, Rupert had given the case much thought. Some disparaging things had been said about him and also about his family and he needed to obtain a private audience with the Prankstons or even with Thomas if he would be willing to such a suggestion, so that he could iron out and explain a few things. Little did Rupert know that Thomas had also been searching for him and now it seemed that their paths were about to collide like stars in a galaxy. Up to the trial, Rupert had been denied access to the Prankston family whilst the case was being heard and the evidence being gathered in order to keep things clinical and not prejudice the outcome of the case. But now that the case was long over and the outcome decided, Rupert hoped that he would be able to obtain an audience with the family who had been deeply scarred by the incident. Rupert believed he understood to some extent the nature of his pain having lost his father in the most awful way. His desire to meet with the family could only prove beneficial to all parties concerned.

A number of years had passed since the verdict and Rupert's

career had blossomed. He was now a consultant with a large private practice in Central London. He had many leading public parliamentarian figures as patients and he therefore enjoyed a comfortable life, financially anyway. His younger brother George had died having contracted pneumonia, leaving only him and his mother who had tried to rebuild her life after the war had ended.

His mother had moved in with her son Rupert because her health had deteriorated and she needed support. Rupert was only too happy to have his mother live with him as he had yet to marry and therefore life could often be lonely. He'd had girlfriends in the past but no-one he had really fallen in love with or who had met with his high expectations. Rupert was a hard man to please when it came to love.

There was still some misgivings and sometimes, only sometimes, Rupert had days when he found it hard to settle his mind over Thomas despite the fact that the tribunal had awarded him handsomely from the Medical Compensation Fund. What made it worse for him was seeing Thomas a year or two after the verdict. It appeared to be Thomas although Rupert couldn't be sure. The young boy was with his mother and was in a wheelchair. It was thought that Thomas needed a wheelchair because there were days when he struggled with his breathing. It was like a dagger to the heart seeing him and the events of that day and the proceedings surrounding the tribunal would resurface again thereby sending Rupert back into the dark moods he so tried to cleanse himself from. Counselling helped to a certain extent but true closure had not been secured. Rupert therefore sought the advice of his friends and his mother too and took what some would say was a hard decision, which was to locate Thomas, who would be a teenager now. Rupert believed there was a lot to be gained from the principles of redemptive and restorative justice.

He was aware that Thomas's mother had spiralled into a deep state of depression and to some extent felt duty bound to assist in whatever way he could. Perhaps support had been lacking or not forthcoming as it should have been. The financial award had helped but emotionally the scars were still visible perhaps more so because the evidence of what happened presented itself daily in the inadequacies faced by Thomas. Every parent has expectations for their child, some realistic and others unrealistic.

For Thomas, it was unfair for Dr. Rupert to be held to ransom for a mistake that could have cost his career. After careful consideration and talking things over with his mother, Thomas decided to pluck up the courage and try and arrange a meeting with Dr. Rupert but only if his mother came along too. His mother agreed.

Sunday 15th of September. It was a day that neither Thomas, his mother or Dr. Rupert, would ever forget in a long while. Thomas decided that he had sufficient information to follow through on his plan to meet with Dr. Rupert. He knew where he worked and in which ward, and he had been making clandestine soundings to work out when Dr. Rupert would most likely be on duty. It was a no brainer really, as both Dr. Rupert and Thomas had surreptitiously and unbeknownst to each other been yearning to meet with one another.

However, the plan which Thomas and his mother were about to embark on was both unorthodox and unrehearsed.

Caroline, Thomas' mother, had reason to visit The Pendlebury Hospital as she had an elderly sister-in- law Annie, who had cancer of the throat and was being treated there. Visiting times took place between 10-12 midday and 2-5pm. It had been noted to Thomas through his connections that Dr. Rupert was due to be doing his ward rounds at around 2:30pm in the neighbouring medical ward.

'Hi Mother,' Thomas said. 'Dr. Rupert is rumoured to be on

duty at around 2pm today. We should telephone my aunt who should be on duty around this time and see if we can perhaps try and sneak a conversation with him.'

'Aunt Anne on duty on the same ward as Dr. Rupert? This is a Godsend.'

'Sure isn't a coincidence,' said Thomas. 'I'm itching to get this all over with. We've come this far and closure must happen today.'

'I'm with you,' his mother said.

'So that settles it then,' he replied. 'Today is the day.' So promptly at 1.30pm both Thomas and his mother clamoured into the pre-booked taxi and made their way to the hospital which was a mere fifteen minutes away.

'All nervous and choked up, I am,' Thomas said quietly to his mother.
'You needn't be', his mother replied. It is your given right to know..... and it will help you move forward with your life,' she continued.

'Mmm, you're right. It is what is needed,' said Thomas,

closure..................so a new chapter can begin. I feel like I've been cocooned in a cell for all of twenty-four years and it is time to make that release and move on. Right, I'm ready,' exhaled Thomas deeply as they both stepped out of the taxi and climbed the few steps into the hospital. Both stood there looking at each other and wondering if they were both doing the right thing.

'Ready.... let's do it,' said Caroline.

'Well it is 2:20pm so we better get our skates on. It would be the ideal thing to apprehend him calmly before he enters the ward, perhaps while he is walking down the corridor,' Thomas said.

'Now that would be an opportune moment,' Caroline said.

They took the lift to the second floor and turned right at the corridor to make their way towards the end of the corridor where the Neonatal Ward was situated. As they walked, a familiar figure came around the corridor and almost collided with him. Thomas gulped and tugged at his mother's sleeve.

'It's him..........'

'Who?' his mother replied.

'Dr. Rupert,' Thomas said.

'How do you know it is him....................you've got to be sure,' his mother said sternly.

'Come on, I have been studying him and carrying out research on him for the past nine months...............I should recognize him by now,' Thomas responded. And with that, Thomas bolted across the pathway, not bothering to see whether his mother had followed him. He tapped Dr. Rupert on the shoulder.

'Hello, I am Thomas Prankston and you are Dr. Rupert, the doctor who assisted at my birth,' said Thomas boldly. Please do not be alarmed, I am not here to accuse you, I just want to talk,' Thomas continued.

'Oh my Lord,' exclaimed Dr. Rupert. Thomas, Thomas, Thomas Prankston,' Dr. Rupert said aloud.

'Yes, this is he,' Thomas replied.

'I was wondering if I would ever get the chance to meet with you and yes, I would like to talk. I have a ward round in about twenty-five minutes but we can speak now,' Dr Rupert said. 'Is now a good time?'

It happened so quick, neither of them had time to catch their breath. No-one really knew how they would react if they got the chance to meet but there was no time to consider feelings or anything. Here was the perfect moment and all parties were happy to talk. By this time, Caroline had joined them. She had expected fireworks but it was just calm. Dr. Rupert extended his hand to Caroline and said,

'You must be his mother, Caroline Prankston. I am so sorry about what happened. I am sorry,' he continued.............

Let's find somewhere to sit and we can talk properly,' Caroline ventured.

'Yes, there is a coffee shop on the first floor, we can go there if you like,' he replied.

'That sounds like a good idea,' Caroline said.

So all three took the lift to the first floor. They found a quiet corner in the cafe and talked for what seemed like ages. Both parties were courteous with each other and listened intently to one another. Considering the horrible things that had been said about Dr. Rupert, it was plain for both Thomas and Caroline to see that he had suffered immensely and this information helped erase some of the pent up anguish and pain they had fostered over the years. The room fell silent after everyone had said what they wanted and they looked around at each other. They all had tears in their eyes. It was a moment of great relief for all three.

'Can I say something?' asked Thomas.

'Yes, say on,' replied Dr. Rupert.

'I know a lot of horrible things have been said about you but we consider,' Thomas said, turning to his mother as he spoke, 'that there is more good to be gained by forgiving rather than perpetually embracing the pain of "what, why and who is to blame."'

Nodding his head, Dr. Rupert wept silently and responded in a somewhat stilted voice. 'I know you have both been deeply scarred by the misgivings of that day and for that I am truly sorry. I would like to offer any help I can. I long hoped for an opportunity like this to occur and appreciate that we have been able to speak so openly and with such candour. I accept the blame but I am truly glad that you are able to forgive. If I could have turned back the clock, I would but................'

'Please.............. don't torture yourself anymore,' Caroline said.

Thomas nodded in agreement. 'We have a better understanding and a fuller picture about the whole event and the mitigating circumstances leading up to that day. We forgive...........wholeheartedly.' Caroline said with tears in her eyes. And she meant it.

'Yes, we do,' Thomas responded.

'Thank you,' Dr. Rupert said quietly.

'We have both been made aware of the positive contribution you have made to medicine and agree that those contributions outweigh all of the negative things that have been written about you,' Caroline said.

Dr. Rupert smiled, and said softly, 'I am just doing my job and a job I love immensely. It is all the more worthwhile when one's efforts are recognized. Thank you. I need to go now,' he said as a message could be heard on the tannoy asking for Dr. Rupert to contact the children's ward.

'Yes, we understand. Thank you for agreeing to see us and sorry if it appeared that we were abrupt at first,' Caroline said.

'Yes, thank you,' Thomas said. It feels like a weight has fallen off my shoulders.' And with that, they all rose up from their seats, hugged, and shook hands.

Walking back to get the lift to the second floor, Dr. Rupert was in reflective mode. People think as doctors that we are invincible but if only they knew that we go through the same symptoms, stresses, and heartaches just like anyone else. Sometimes the pressures put upon us as medics are insurmountable. We are after all only human.

Thomas and Caroline made their way to the taxi rank. 'This is no petty case of right or wrong, it is more involved than that,' said Thomas, reflecting on their conversation earlier with Dr. Rupert.

'Listen Mother,' Thomas gestured, 'In a war where fifteen million would die and twenty million would be wounded, to hold an eternal grudge against one is unjust!'

'Such compassion....' Caroline said, 'and such kindness...... the world would be a better place if only they could adopt the same principles...........'

'Yes indeed,' Thomas replied with a smile.

Dedications

This book is first and foremost dedicated to my **Mother** whom I loved daily and shared many a fond moment with. She would be delighted that this book has been published. I miss her daily and her wisdom.

This book is also dedicated to my brother **Donovan Alexander Skyers**, a much loved brother confidante and friend…..gone way too soon.

A big thank you to my Illustrator Ian Melling and his team.

Printed in Great Britain
by Amazon

81541129R00061